The Hungry Donkey

Heather Amery

Illustrated by Stephen Cartwright

Language consultant: Betty Root
Series editor: Jenny Tyler

There is a little yellow duck to find on every page.

This is Apple Tree Farm.

This is Mrs. Boot, the farmer. She has two children, called Poppy and Sam, and a dog called Rusty.

There is a donkey on the farm.

The donkey is called Ears. She lives in a field
with lots of grass, but she is always hungry.

Ears, the donkey, is going out.

Poppy and Sam catch Ears and take her to the farmyard. Today is the day of the Show.

Ears has a little cart.

They brush her coat, comb her tail and clean
her feet. Mrs. Boot puts her into her little cart.

Off they go to the Show.

Poppy and Sam climb up into the cart. They
all go down the lane to the show ground.

"You stay here, Ears."

At the show ground, Mrs. Boot ties Ears to a fence. "Stay here. We'll be back soon," she says.

Ears gets free.

Ears is hungry and bored with nothing to do.
She pulls and pulls on the rope until she is free.

Ears looks for food.

Ears trots across the field to the show ring.
She sees a bunch of flowers and some fruit.

"That looks good to eat."

She takes a big bite, but the flowers do not taste very nice. A lady screams and Ears is frightened.

Ears runs away.

Mrs. Boot, Poppy and Sam and the lady run
after her and catch her.

"Naughty donkey," says Sam.

"I'm sorry," Mrs. Boot says to the lady. "Would you like to take Ears to the best donkey competition?"

Ears is very good now.

The lady is called Mrs. Rose. She climbs into the cart. "Come on," she says, and shakes the reins.

Ears pulls the cart into the show ring.

She trots in front of the judges. She stops and goes when Mrs. Rose tells her.

Ears wins a prize.

"Well done," says the judge, giving her a rosette.
He gives Mrs. Rose a prize too. It is a hat.

It is time to go home.

Mrs. Rose waves goodbye. "That was such fun,"
she says. Ears trots home. She has a new hat too.

Cover design by Hannah Ahmed   Digital manipulation by Sarah Cronin

This edition first published in 2004 by Usborne Publishing Ltd, 83-85 Saffron Hill, London EC1N 8RT, England. www.usborne.com